COUNTRIES IN THE NEWS

MEXICO

Kieran Walsh

Publishing LLC
Vero Beach, Florida 32964

© 2005 Rourke Publishing LLC

All rights reserved. No part of this book may be reproduced or utilized in any form or by any means, electronic or mechanical including photocopying, recording, or by any information storage and retrieval system without permission in writing from the publisher.

www.rourkepublishing.com

The country's flag is correct at the time of going to press.

PHOTO CREDITS: ©Susana Gonzalez/Newsmakers Cover;
All other images ©Peter Langer Associated Media Group

Title page: *Children in the Mexican state of Quintana Roo*

Editor: Frank Sloan

Cover and interior design by Nicola Stratford

Library of Congress Cataloging-in-Publication Data

Walsh, Kieran.
  Mexico / Kieran Walsh.
     p. cm. -- (Countries in the news II)
  Includes bibliographical references and index.
  ISBN 1-59515-176-1 (hardcover)
  1. Mexico--Juvenile literature. I. Title. II. Series: Walsh, Kieran. Countries in the news II.
  F1208.5.W35 2004
  972--dc22
                              2004009686

Printed in the USA

CG/CG

TABLE OF CONTENTS

Welcome to Mexico 4

The People 8

Life in Mexico 12

School and Sports 14

Food and Holidays 16

The Future 19

Fast Facts 20

Crossing Borders 21

Glossary 22

Further Reading 23

Websites to Visit 23

Index 24

WELCOME TO MEXICO

Mexico is a country just south of the United States. Mexico comes into contact with four states: Texas, New Mexico, Arizona, and California. Bodies of water like the Pacific Ocean and The Gulf of Mexico surround Mexico on both sides.

A cruise ship moors in the bay of Acapulco

Most of Mexico is made up of the Mexican **Plateau**. This land area extends from Mexico's border with the United States nearly to the Yucatan **Peninsula** in the southeast. Mexico has several major rivers. The most famous of these is the Rio Grande.

The Rio Grande begins in Colorado and flows south following the border between Texas and Mexico.

Mexico is a warm place. In the months of April and May, the average temperature hovers around 80° F (26.7° C).

The capital of Mexico, Mexico City, is one of the largest cities in the world. It also happens to be one of the oldest. Built by the Spanish, Mexico City is located on top of the ruins of a city once known as Tenochtitlán.

A model of the ancient city of Tenochtitlán

A view of Mexico City from the air

THE PEOPLE

The largest portion of the Mexican population, about 60 percent, are **mestizos**—meaning they are of mixed race. Mexican mestizos are a combination of American Indian **ancestry** mixed with Spanish or Portuguese.

An artisan puts finishing touches to his work.

Children enjoy a frosty treat.

About 30 percent of the Mexican population is **Amerindian**. Amerindians primarily live in the Mexican countryside. More than 50 Indian languages are still spoken in Mexico, including Mixtec, Otomi, Tarascan, and Zapotec.

Most mestizos live in Mexico's cities.

Most Mexicans (about 89 percent) are Roman Catholic, but there are a small number of Protestants—around 6 percent.

Although some Mexicans live in the countryside and work on farms, about 75 percent of the population lives and works in cities. This is part of the reason why Mexico City is the most heavily populated city in the world after Tokyo.

Fishermen haul their catch on shore.

10

The famous divers jump from the cliffs near Acapulco.

LIFE IN MEXICO

A mariachi player entertains in city streets.

Many aspects of Mexican life are probably already familiar to you. The word **mariachi**, for instance, describes a type of music. It is usually performed in public spaces by wandering musicians in traditional costumes.

Young boys in Cholula, in the state of Puebla

Mexico City's cathedral and the zócalo

Often, mariachi music is the accompaniment for Mexican dancing.

While movies and television are popular in Mexico, just as much time is spent visiting with friends and socializing. Typically, this is done in the **zócalo**, or town square, on a Sunday afternoon.

SCHOOL AND SPORTS

School attendance is required for Mexican children between the ages of 6 and 14. From the ages of 6 to 11, children attend elementary school. After this, they move on to three years at a basic secondary school. Then, students have the option to attend upper secondary school followed by college.

Parasailing at Acapulco

A matador and bull compete at the Plaza de Toros in Mexico City.

American sports such as baseball are popular in Mexico. Also very popular, though, are Spanish sports such as bullfighting. In fact, the Monumental Plaza Mexico in Mexico City is the largest bullfighting ring in the world, seating up to 60,000 people.

The **literacy** rate in Mexico is 90 percent.

FOOD AND HOLIDAYS

You have almost certainly tasted Mexican food. Salsa, refried beans, tacos… all of these Mexican favorites probably spring to mind. However, Mexican cooking also includes many dishes you may not be familiar with, like **menudo** (seafood soup), beef stew, and rice salad.

A fisherman sets his nets. His catch will be used in many typical dishes.

A cook grills tacos outdoors.

Probably the most important of all Mexican holidays is Cinco de Mayo, which means "The Fifth of May." This date marks the anniversary of a battle between France and Mexico. Another very important day is Dieciséis de Septiembre, or September 16. It was on September 16, 1810, that Mexico began a war with Spain for **independence**.

One way to travel in Mexico City is by pedicab.

THE FUTURE

Mexico is not without its problems. Mexico City is very overcrowded, and many of the people who live there do not have sewage facilities.

Pollution in Mexico City is also a serious problem. This is partly a result of the number of cars in the city, and the fact that Mexico City is surrounded by mountains that do not allow polluted air to escape.

However, people are looking for solutions for these problems. For instance, the Mexican government has been experimenting with a plan to have one day every week when people don't drive their cars. It is likely that Mexico will remain an important country for many years to come.

FAST FACTS

Area: 761,602 square miles (1,972,307 sq km)

Borders: The United States to the north; Belize and Guatemala in the southeast

Population: 104,907,991

Monetary Unit: Mexican peso

Largest Cities: Mexico City, Ecatepec, Guadalajara, Puebla, Nezahualcóyotl, Monterrey

Government: Federal Republic

Religion: nominally Roman Catholic 89%, Protestant 6%, other 5%

Crops: Corn, wheat, soybeans, rice, beans, cotton, coffee, fruit, tomatoes

Natural Resources: Petroleum, silver, copper, gold, lead, zinc, natural gas, timber

Major Industries: Tobacco, chemicals, iron and steel, petroleum, mining, textiles, clothing, motor vehicles, consumer durables, tourism

CROSSING BORDERS

In order for people from another country to become citizens of the United States, they must go through a process called **naturalization**. Many Mexicans, though, live and work in the United States without becoming naturalized.

Mexico is directly connected to the United States. This makes it easy for people to cross the borders that separate the two countries. Although the U.S. government has taken steps to increase security along the border with Mexico, people are often able to enter into the United States illegally.

GLOSSARY

Amerindian (AM eh rin dee un) — an American Indian

ancestry (AN sess tree) — a person's family history

independence (IN duh PEN dents) — freedom; self-rule

literacy (LIT er uh see) — the ability to read and write

mariachi (MARE ee atch ee) — a Mexican street band

menudo (meh NOO doh) — seafood soup

mestizos (meh STEE zos) — Mexicans of American Indian and either Spanish or Portuguese descent

naturalization (natch er eh la zay shun) — the process by which a person from another country becomes an American citizen

peninsula (pe NIN suh lah) — a land mass that is surrounded by water on three sides

plateau (plah TOE) — a flat, elevated area

pollution (puh LOO shun) — dirty air or water

zócalo (ZOH cal oh) — a town square

FURTHER READING

Find out more about Mexico with these helpful books:

- Asher, Sandy. *Mexico: Discovering Cultures.* Benchmark Books, 2003
- Cobb, Allan B. *Mexico: A Primary Source Cultural Guide.* Rosen Publishing Group, 2003
- Goodwin, William. *Mexico: Modern Nations of the World.* Lucent Books, 1999
- Hamilton, Janice. *Visual Geography: Mexico in Pictures.* Lerner Publications, 2003
- Park, Ted. *Taking Your Camera to Mexico.* Steadwell Books, 2000
- Reilly, Mary Jo and Leslie Jermyn. *Cultures of the World: Mexico.* Benchmark Books, 2002

WEBSITES TO VISIT

- www.infoplease.com/ipa/A0107779.html
  Infoplease – Mexico
- gomexico.about.com/index.htm?terms=Mexico
  About.com – Mexico/Central America for Visitors

INDEX

Amerindian 9
bullfighting 15
Cinco de Mayo 17
Gulf of Mexico 4
mariachi 12, 13
menudo 16
mestizos 8, 9
Mexican Plateau 5
Mexico City 6, 10, 15, 19
naturalization 21
Pacific Ocean 4
pollution 19
Portuguese 8
Rio Grande 5
Spain 17
Spanish 6, 8
Tenochtitlán 6
Yucatan 5
zócalo 13

About the Author

Kieran Walsh is a writer of children's nonfiction books, primarily on historical and social studies topics. Walsh has been involved in the children's book field as editor, proofreader, and illustrator as well as author.

SEP 14 2005